little Tumbo

little Tumbo

written and illustrated by **Steven Salerno**

MARSHALL CAVENDISH

Tumbo was small for an elephant, but he knew that one day he'd be **BIG** just like his mother and father.

Whenever Tumbo tried to trumpet, a little squeak came out.
It made his older sister laugh.

"Squeak, squeak, squeak!" she teased.

This made Tumbo angry.

He would take a deep breath, raise his trunk, and blow
as hard as he could. **Squeeeak!**

Tumbo practiced every day, but it didn't help.

"I'll never be able to trumpet!" he whined.

"Someday soon," comforted his father with a smile.

During the hot afternoons, the family rested together in the shade of the Bungalis trees.

One afternoon, they settled down for a nap, but Tumbo
was *not* sleepy. He fidgeted when his mother tried to pull
him close to her.

Tumbo wanted to explore.

"Do not wander far!" his mother warned with a yawn.

Tumbo didn't listen.

In the distance, he spotted a tasty red fruit hanging from a tree and went for a closer look.

When Tumbo reached out to pick the red fruit, a tall thin hunter leaped out from his hiding place and shoved the little elephant right into a waiting cage. A stubby hunter snapped the door shut!

Tumbo tried to trumpet, but his frightened squeaks for help were not loud enough to wake his napping family. The hunters were swift and soon had carried Tumbo far away from the shade of the Bungalis trees.

The tall hunter bent down and peered into the cage.

"You'll fetch a nice price at the market, little one!" he snickered.

Oh, how Tumbo cried! He wanted to be back with his family, safe once again.

They came to a wide river, where an old man and his grandson ferried people across in their flatboat.

"Not a peep, if you know what's good for you!" the tall hunter said to Tumbo.

He placed a blanket over Tumbo's cage.

As the boat made its way across the river, the old boatman began to lift the blanket off Tumbo's cage.

"Leave it be, old man!" yelled the stubby hunter. So the old boatman stepped back and said nothing.

After crossing the river, the hunters continued to carry Tumbo away. Into the jungle they went, following a path through the giant leaves and heading up the mountain.

When night fell, Tumbo shivered inside his cage.

"Tomorrow morning, we will be rid of you!" shouted the tall hunter.

"We'll sell you to the highest bidder!" added the stubby hunter.

"Maybe you will end up working in a circus!" he howled.

The hunters let the campfire burn down, rolled out their blankets, and soon were snoring loudly.

Tumbo found the brightest star in the sky and made a wish. "I want to be with my family again," he whispered, blinking away the tears. "Please let me see them again!"

Suddenly a small, dark face appeared in the bush next to Tumbo's cage. It was the boy from the riverboat! "*Shhhhhhhhhh,*" he cautioned.

The boy cut the rope holding the cage door and opened it with a C R E A K !

"Follow me!" the boy whispered.
Together they scurried down the mountain
and into the jungle. Tumbo and the boy
ran all through the night and into the
morning, when they stopped to rest by
a stream.

"My grandfather is a wise old man," said the boy.
"He suspected those hunters would sell you at the
marketplace, so he sent me to try and set you free."
Tumbo held the boy's hand with his trunk. It was
his way of saying "thank you."

"Come, little elephant," said the boy. "We must make our way to the river now."

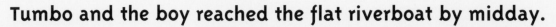

Tumbo and the boy reached the flat riverboat by midday.
"There you are, little elephant!" said the old man with a broad
smile. He kissed his grandson and then quickly ferried the boat
back across the river.

On the other side, Tumbo hopped off.
"Good-bye little friend," shouted the old man. "Now hurry straight
home to your family!"

Tumbo tried to trumpet a thank-you to the old man and his grandson . . . but, as usual, it came out as a squeak.
Then he headed toward home to find his family.

SQUEAK!

The sun was hot as he walked, and Tumbo was thirsty.
His little feet were sore.
That night Tumbo rested by a small pool of water.

In the morning, Tumbo set out again as fast as he could. He was getting closer to home now!

On top of the next ridge, Tumbo stopped. There in the distance he spotted his mother and father, sister—his aunts, uncles, and cousins too!

Tumbo was about to run to them when he felt a rope around his legs!

"Did you think you could run away from us?" sneered the tall thin hunter. The stubby hunter pulled the rope tighter.

"OUCH!" cried Tumbo. He tried to wiggle and twist free.

The hunters hoisted Tumbo off the
ground and began to carry him away.
"Back to the marketplace for you,"
they bellowed.

Tumbo closed his eyes, took a deep breath,
raised his trunk, and . . . S Q U E A K E D !
"No one can hear your baby squeaks,"
the stubby hunter said with a laugh.
Tumbo was terrified!

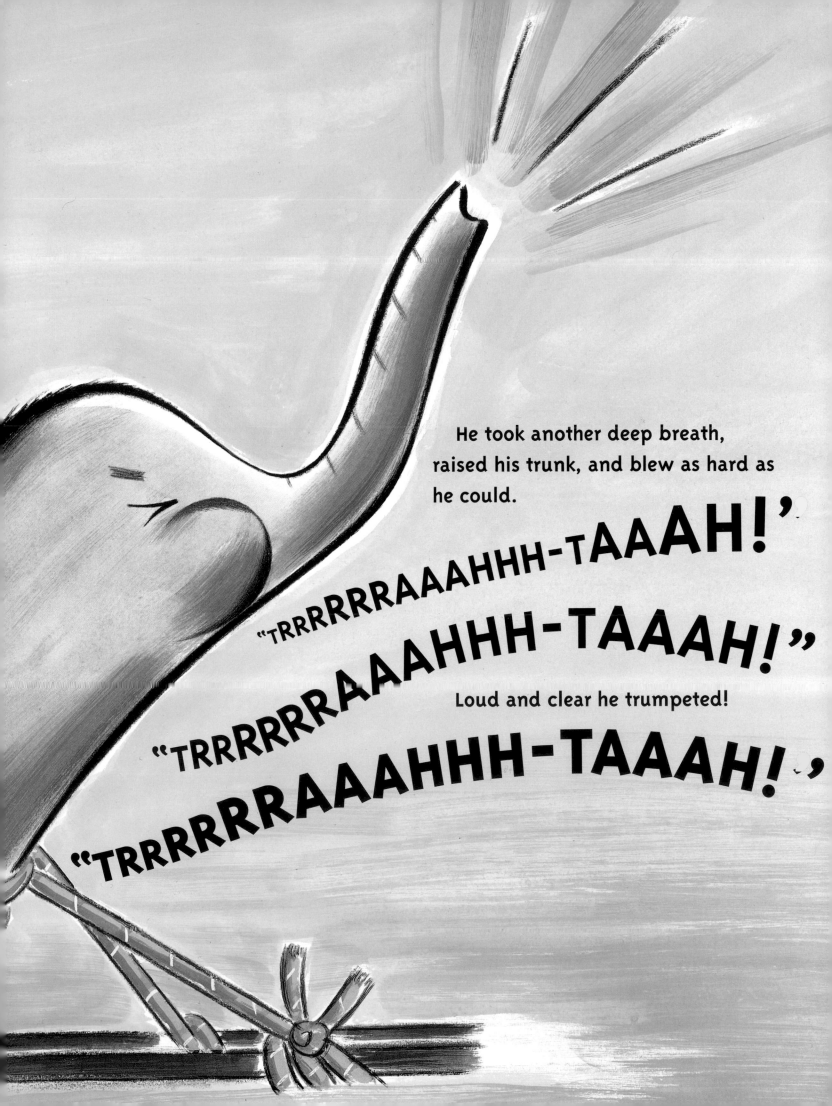

He took another deep breath, raised his trunk, and blew as hard as he could.

"TRRRRRAAAHHH-TAAAH!"

"TRRRRRAAAHHH-TAAAH!"

Loud and clear he trumpeted!

"TRRRRRAAAHHH-TAAAH!"

The ground began to tremble and shake like an earthquake!
Over the ridge Tumbo's entire family appeared, with Mother
and Father in the lead!

"TRRRRRRAAAHHH-TAAAH!"

they all trumpeted to Tumbo in return.

When the two hunters saw all the **BIG** elephants thundering toward them, they quickly dropped Tumbo and ran away as fast as they could!

Tumbo's mother, father, sister, aunts, uncles, and cousins surrounded him. They untied the ropes and hugged him. Mother held Tumbo tight and kissed him.

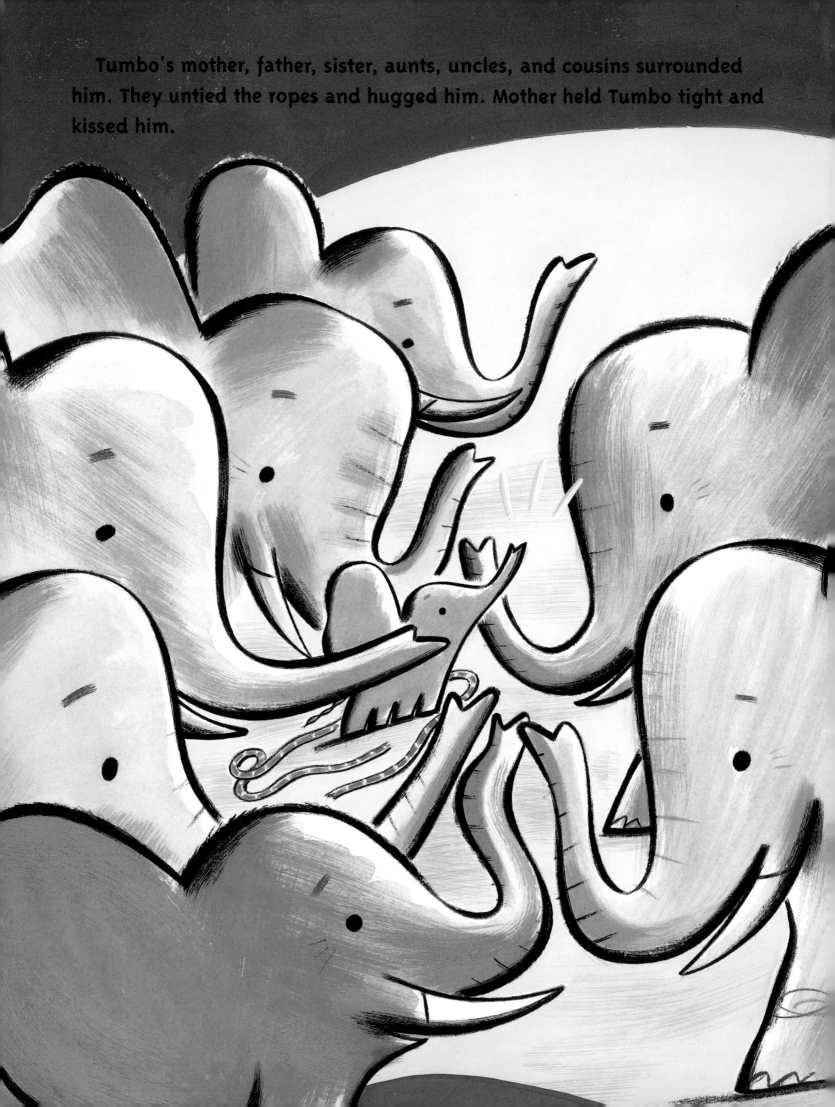

"I can trumpet!" shouted Tumbo. "I can TRUMPET!"
Father smiled proudly, giving Tumbo a nudge.

"TRRRRRAAAHHH-TAAAH!"

Tumbo blasted a trumpet
into his sister's ear!

They all walked home together. In the afternoon, when the sun was hot, the family rested in the shade of the Bungalis trees, just as before.

"Do not wander far!" his mother warned Tumbo with a yawn.

Marshall Cavendish
99 White Plains Road
Tarrytown, NY 10591
www.marshallcavendish.com

Text and illustrations copyright © 2003 by Steven Salerno

The text of this book is set in 17-point Tripley
The illustrations are rendered in watercolor and gouache.

Library of Congress Cataloging-in-Publication Data

Salerno, Steven.
Little Tumbo / written and illustrated by Steven Salerno.— 1st ed.
p. cm.
Summary: When a baby elephant named Little Tumbo is captured by hunters,
he wishes he could trumpet loudly to summon help.

ISBN 0-7614-5136-6

[1. Elephants—Fiction.] I. Title.
PZ7.S15212 Li 2003
[E]—dc21
2002154278

Printed in China

First edition
2 4 6 8 7 5 3 1